# DISNEY'S MULAN

Illustrated by the Disney Storybook Artists
Story adapted by Amy Adair

© Disney Enterprises, Inc.

Published by
Louis Weber, C.E.O.
Publications International, Ltd.
7373 North Cicero Avenue
Lincolnwood, Illinois 60712

**www.pilbooks.com**

Manufactured in China.

8 7 6 5 4 3 2 1

ISBN: 0-7853-9769-8

Long ago a girl named Mulan lived in a small village in China. She was very beautiful. But she was also very smart and brave. Mulan's family wanted nothing more than for Mulan to find a husband to uphold the family honor. Today was the day that she was going to meet her matchmaker.

Mulan wanted to make a good impression, so she practiced reciting all the qualities that made a good wife.

"Let's see," Mulan said. "Quiet, graceful, and punctual." She knew she would never remember the entire list, so she painted the words on her arm.

She did not want to forget a single thing.

"Mulan!" her father yelled. "You should be in town. We're counting on you to uphold the family honor."

Mulan raced to town. Her mother and grandmother were already there, waiting for Mulan to arrive.

They wanted Mulan to look perfect when she met the Matchmaker. They pulled and tugged on her hair until it was just right. Then they helped her into a beautiful dress.

Mulan was ready to meet the Matchmaker. She was as pretty as a porcelain doll, but she did not feel like herself.

"Fa Mulan," the Matchmaker called.

"Present," Mulan said, raising her hand.

"Speaking without permission," the Matchmaker scolded. She examined Mulan.

"Too skinny," mumbled the Matchmaker. "Now tell me, what makes a good wife?"

Mulan remembered the list that she had practiced over and over. She glanced at the writing on her arm. Some of the ink had started to run, so it was difficult to read. "You should fulfill your duties calming and respectively. Reflect before you snack," she said, reading her arm. "I mean act. This shall bring you honor and glory."

The Matchmaker grabbed Mulan's arm, smearing the ink all over her own hand. Then the Matchmaker raised her hand and accidentally smeared the ink on her face, too.

"Now pour the tea," the Matchmaker ordered
Mulan. Cri-Kee, Mulan's lucky cricket, hopped into the
tea. It spilled all down the Matchmaker's dress. *Crash!*
The Matchmaker then tripped over a chair.

"You are a disgrace," the angry Matchmaker said to
Mulan. "You may look like a bride, but you will never
bring your family honor."

Mulan's father saw that she was very sad. He gave her a hug. He loved Mulan.

*Boom, boom, boom!* They heard drums in the distance. "What is it?" Mulan asked.

"Go inside," her mother ordered.

A messenger rode his horse into the center of the village. "Citizens! The Huns have invaded China!" the messenger told the villagers. "By order of the Emperor, one man from each family must serve in the army."

Mulan did not have a brother, so her father had to serve. But her father could barely walk without using his crutch.

Mulan knew he could never fight in a battle.

"Father, you can't go!" Mulan yelled.

"Silence!" the messenger ordered. "You should teach your daughter to be silent when there is a man present."

"Mulan," her father said, turning away from her. "You dishonor me."

"Report to the Wu Zhong camp tomorrow," the messenger said, handing Mulan's father the Emperor's orders.

Mulan watched as her father tried to walk while holding his heavy sword. He fell down. He was too weak to join the Emperor's army. She had to do something.

Mulan begged him not to go. "You shouldn't have to join," she cried. "There are plenty of young men."

But her father was a proud man. He did not listen to any of her pleas. "It is an honor to protect my family and country," he said.

She could not let him go. Mulan decided that she would disguise herself as a man and take his place. Late that night, she cut off her beautiful long black hair. Then she stole her father's armor.

Mulan knew she had to protect her father. In the middle of the night, she rode off on a horse to join the Emperor's army. When her family discovered that she was missing, they called upon the spirits of their ancestors to protect Mulan.

The Great Ancestor and a teeny-tiny dragon named Mushu were the first to awaken. Mushu was excited to help Mulan's family. But the Great Ancestor reminded him that he was not allowed to protect any of the family members. His job was just to awaken the other ancestors.

"We must send a real dragon to help Mulan," the Great Ancestor said. "Go awaken the Great Stone Dragon."

Mushu was disappointed. He grabbed his gong and jumped on the big stone statue's shoulder. When he banged his gong, the Great Stone Dragon crumbled to pieces! All that was left was the Stone Dragon's head and a heap of rocks.

Mushu did not want to let Mulan and the other ancestors down. He decided he would make Mulan a war hero. Not only would he help Mulan, but he'd finally prove himself to the ancestors.

Cri-Kee hopped along and chirped that he was lucky as he and Mushu set off on their journey to find Mulan.

Mulan was nervous as she rested on her way to the soldiers' camp. She was sure the other soldiers would know right away that she was a girl.

Suddenly there was a hot blast of fire. Gigantic flames shot out in front of her. The shadow of a huge dragon appeared in the middle of the flames. "I am the guardian of lost souls!" Mushu bellowed. "Your ancestors sent me to protect you." With that, the fire went out, and Mushu stood in front of Mulan.

"My ancestors sent a little lizard to help me?" Mulan asked Mushu.

"I'm a dragon!" Mushu shouted.

"You're tiny," Mulan said. Mulan could see that she had hurt Mushu's feelings. "I'm sorry," she said. "I'm just a little nervous. I have never done this before."

"You have to trust me," Mushu said. They soon arrived at the soldiers' camp. Mulan walked just like Mushu told her to. She held her head up high and strutted. She hoped she looked like a real solider.

Suddenly all of the soldiers started to fight, and Mulan was right in the middle of it.

"Soldiers!" Captain Li Shang shouted. "I do not need trouble in my camp. What is your name?" He pointed right at Mulan.

"My name is Ping," Mulan said. She handed Captain Li Shang her father's orders to serve.

It was Captain Li Shang's job to train the men to fight the Huns. He shot an arrow, and it landed at the top of a very tall pole. Each man tried to reach it. Then it was Mulan's turn. Just like the others, she could not even climb halfway up the pole. Then Captain Li Shang gave each man some weights to carry. They started to run. Mulan could not keep up. She dropped her weights and fell down.

"Pack up and go home," Li Shang said. "I could never make a soldier out of you."

Mulan remembered her family. She wanted to honor her father. As the men returned to camp, Mulan followed behind. She tried to reach the arrow one last time.

Using her head instead of her strength, Mulan looped the weights together and used them as a brace to hoist herself to the top. She climbed higher and higher until she finally reached the top. Mulan grabbed the arrow and threw it down to the ground. The arrow landed right in front of Captain Li Shang.

All the men cheered for Mulan! She proved she could become a very good soldier.

Soon, Mulan and the other troops traveled up a snow covered mountain. Suddenly they found themselves completely surrounded by the enemy! Mulan had an idea. She aimed a cannon at the snow-capped mountain.

*Bang!* A cannonball blasted into the mountain. The mountain began to shake, causing an avalanche. Mulan saved her entire unit, but she was badly wounded.

When the doctor examined Mulan, he discovered her secret. She was a girl! The captain and the rest of the army were stunned. They left Mulan behind.

"I should have never left home," Mulan told Mushu.

Mushu hung his head. "You were just trying to help someone you loved. I was just trying to help myself," Mushu admitted. "Your ancestors did not send me. They don't even like me."

Cri-Kee chirped.

"What?" Mushu asked Cri-Kee. "What do you mean you're not lucky?"

"I will have to face my father sooner or later," Mulan said. "Let's go home."

Suddenly Mulan heard something strange. She looked down the mountain. Shan-Yu, the leader of the Huns, was still alive! "I have to do something," Mulan said. She raced to the Imperial City.

Everyone in the city was celebrating Captain Li Shang's victory. "Li Shang!" Mulan yelled. "The Huns are in the Imperial City!"

"Go home," Li Shang ordered Mulan. "You do not belong here."

Mulan tried to warn the Emperor's guards, but they wouldn't listen to her, either. Suddenly the Huns captured the Emperor. They dragged him into the palace and locked the doors.

Li Shang and his soldiers tried to break down the door, but it was too strong.

"I have an idea," Mulan said to the soldiers. They followed Mulan, and she disguised them all as women.

Then they climbed
the poles in front of the palace,
just like they had learned in camp.
They tricked the guards and reached the Emperor
just in time. Shan-Yu was furious. He wanted revenge.

Mulan had another idea. She leaped up on the roof.
Shan-Yu followed her. Mushu and Cri-Kee raced to a
tower that launched fireworks.

*Pop! Pop! Pop!* A giant rocket guided by Mushu
knocked Shan-Yu off the roof. Mulan saved the Emperor
and the Imperial City.

The entire crowd cheered for Mulan. She was a hero.
She had saved China! The Emperor gave Mulan his crest
and Shan-Yu's sword. Mulan knew it was finally time for
her to go home.

"These are from the Emperor," Mulan said when she arrived at home. "They are to honor the family."

Mulan's father took the gifts. Then he set them down and hugged Mulan. "The greatest gift and honor is having you for a daughter," he said. "I've missed you so much."

Li Shang also missed Mulan. He had grown to respect and care for her, so he traveled to her home.

Mulan was so happy. But she knew she could not have saved China without her friend, Mushu.

"Thank you," she said, giving Mushu a hug. Mulan had learned that friendship is one of life's greatest honors.